# TWICE TOLD TALES

Twicetold Tales is published by Stone Arch Books
A Capstone Imprint
1710 Roe Crest Drive
North Mankato, Minnesota 56003
www.capstonepub.com

Library of Congress Cataloging-in-Publication Data
Snowe, Olivia, author.
  Hansen and Gracie / by Olivia Snowe; illustrated by
Michelle Lamoreaux.
     pages cm. -- (Twicetold tales)
  Summary: Hansen and Gracie are orphaned twins,
but their ability to hear each other even when they are
not together has made them strange, and prevented
them from being adopted--so when the evil officials
from the orphanage abandon them in the woods, they
set out to find a home of their own.
  ISBN 978-1-4342-9146-2 (library binding) -- ISBN
978-1-4342-9831-7 (paper over board) -- ISBN 978-1-
4342-9150-9 (pbk.) -- ISBN 978-1-4965-0083-0 (ebook)
1. Hansel and Gretel (Tale)--Juvenile fiction. 2. Fairy
tales. 3. Orphans--Juvenile fiction. 4. Twins--Juvenile
fiction. 5. Brothers and sisters--Juvenile fiction.
6. Witches--Juvenile fiction. 7. Psychic ability--Juvenile
fiction. [1. Fairy tales. 2. Orphans--Fiction. 3. Twins--
Fiction. 4. Brothers and sisters--Fiction. 5. Witches--
Fiction. 6. Psychic ability--Fiction.] I. Lamoreaux,
Michelle, illustrator. II. Title.
  PZ8.S41763Han 2014
813.6--dc23
                              2013045321

Designer: Kay Fraser
Vector Images: Shutterstock

Printed in China.
032014   8116WAIF14

# Hansen
## and Gracie

by Olivia Snowe

illustrated by Michelle Lamoreaux

STONE ARCH BOOKS™

You know the story.

You've heard it before.

Everyone has.

Now, read it again.

A new twist. A new gasp.

The story is told again.

# TWICETOLD.

~1~

It's December at the Lakeview Sunrise Group Home for Boys and Girls. From the caged window next to our dormitory bunk bed, we can see the concrete courtyard covered with fresh snow.

But no one is thinking about Christmas or presents, sledding or huge turkeys in the oven. No one is even thinking about gathering mounds of snow into snowmen, and no one is thinking about igloos and forts.

Not here anyway.

Lakeview Sunrise Group Home for Boys and Girls is really just a long and lovely way of saying "orphanage." And this orphanage is as filthy and overcrowded as anything Little Orphan Annie or Oliver Twist ever knew.

It's nowhere near any lake or stream, unless you count the puddle of sewage overflow that visits the corner of Fifth Street and Roosevelt Avenue each spring.

And you couldn't spot a sunrise from here unless you were standing on top of the boarded-up Hurkemeyer Department Store two blocks over. It's the only way you can see over the other run-down gray and brown buildings.

We should know. We live here.

We are Hansen and Gracie. We are twins. And we hate it here.

We haven't been here forever. That is, we've had other homes before. We don't

remember being born, obviously, because no one does.

We do remember several foster homes . . . here in the city, out in the country. But they blur together, so sometimes Gracie believes the family with the big yellow dog was the one who had tuna casserole every Friday, when in fact, Hansen insists, the big yellow dog was in the house with two dads. Gracie says none of the homes had two moms, and that's where we couldn't agree.

It was all so long ago. We've been in the orphanage—no matter what it reads on the sign outside, we usually call it the orphanage— for almost ten years.

Here's the thing about being raised by the state: if foster home after foster home says there's something strange about you, eventually the state stops trying to find you a home. They stop trying to find you a family.

And they put you in a place like this.

It's on this early, cold winter morning that Gracie, always the one of us most likely to get in trouble, is sneaking around the kitchen, sticking her nose into cupboards and cabinets. She's looking for the food the grown-ups save for themselves.

She does this now and then, though all she's ever managed to find worth snatching was a single banana.

It was the best banana we ever tasted, of course. But still. With the trouble Gracie would get into if she were ever caught, Hansen isn't a huge fan of these expeditions.

"I can't find anything," Gracie whispers into the silent, pre-dawn kitchen, frustrated. She knows there has to be good, fresh bread somewhere in here.

"Then get back here," Hansen murmurs into his pillow.

We're far apart—Hansen up in the dormitory and Gracie deep inside the pantry among sacks of buggy flour, dusty cans of corn and carrots and evaporated milk, and boxes upon boxes of powdered potatoes.

But we can still hear each other. We can always hear each other.

For a long time, we didn't know it was a weird thing. But we eventually realized that not all brothers and sisters were like us. Not even most twins were like us.

It turned out it was not only a weird thing, it was *the* weird thing. That's why we could never stay long in a foster home.

All our foster parents were too weirded out to let us stay more than a month or two. They didn't know why we always answered questions the same way. They didn't understand how we were able to tell them what the other was doing, seeing, hearing, and even thinking at that exact moment. Once they found out about our connection, they threw us out.

But we can't be thrown out of the Lakeview

Sunrise Group Home for Boys and Girls. The orphanage is the last refuge for troublemakers and freaks.

That's why we belong here.

~2~

"I'll be back in a second," Gracie whispers. "I just heard something in the hallway. I think it's Ms. Young."

Ms. Young is the woman who runs this place. She's not as miserable as you might guess. She's nice enough when she's in a good mood, and we think she probably got into the business of running an orphanage for the right reasons.

But it's a miserable job, and things never seem to go as well as grown-ups think they will. Even grown-ups who have the best intentions.

"Oscar is with her," Gracie adds, and Hansen—who could just make out the voices as well, hearing them through Gracie's ears—shivers.

Oscar, as far as we can tell, is some kind of building maintenance man. Or he's supposed to be. But he really only fixes drips and creaks when he gets around to it.

He prefers to spend his time trailing behind Ms. Young, offering advice she doesn't ask for. Unfortunately, Ms. Young is often too meek to ignore his advice, and his advice . . . well, that's what makes the orphanage such an especially unpleasant place.

"Have him sleep next to the boiler for seven nights," Oscar might say when a boy hasn't finished his supper, and Ms. Young will click her tongue and agree, sending the boy to the basement.

"Put her in the courtyard for some quiet time," he might whisper in Ms. Young's ear if a girl's language is foul when she's doing her chores. And off the girl goes, though both grown-ups know very well that the courtyard is infested with rats the size of terriers.

This morning, Gracie huddles deeper into the shelves of food, where she'll never be spotted. She pulls in her knees and holds her breath.

"Get back here," Hansen says, his voice full of worry.

Gracie shakes her head. "I wanna hear what they're talking about," she says. "Besides, they're still in the hall. How would I ever get back?"

Hansen clenches his jaw and grumbles.

"Hush," Gracie says. "I want to listen."

So Hansen hushes, and he strains to hear the conversation, too.

"It's the way they look at everyone," says Ms. Young. "Like they're, I don't know . . ."

Oscar finishes for her, his voice a cruel and raspy whisper, "Like they're watching us on TV."

We can hear the solemn agreement in Ms. Young's voice when she replies, "Yes. Like we're not real. Like we exist only for their morbid amusement."

"It's time to get rid of them, then," Oscar says. His voice is brave now, louder than it should be—not that he knows we are listening to him.

"What does he mean?" Hansen says, and Gracie shushes him again.

The woman clicks her tongue. Her feet shuffle on the old wood floors.

"I've tried," Ms. Young says. "I've really

tried. The two have been in and out of foster homes since their parents passed away."

"Then another won't hurt," Oscar says.

Ms. Young moves into the kitchen. Her clunky footsteps and her ice-cold voice echo off the tile floor and walls.

"I'm afraid it's not that simple," she says. "Some of these children I could place in foster homes, in theory. But these two . . . it's impossible."

"I suppose so," Oscar says, as if he might drop the matter. But then he says, "There might be another way."

Ms. Young stops and leans on the counter. Gracie can see her now, just barely, from her hiding spot in the pantry. "What are you getting at?"

"Have they ever run away?" Oscar says. We can almost see him sneering now, showing off his hyena grin of brownish-yellow, broken teeth.

"Of course," Ms. Young says. "Dozens of times. They're infamous."

"Then they'll run away again, won't they?" he says.

"Who knows," says Ms. Young, her voice slow and sad.

"You misunderstand, ma'am," says Oscar. Gracie sees his feet, in well-worn work boots, move closer to Ms. Young's at the counter. He continues, "So I'll be blunt."

"Go right ahead," she says.

"Tell them they've been adopted," he says, "or that some family is interested in adopting them. Some family miles away from here, mind you."

He carefully paces his words as he speaks, like he fancies himself some sort of criminal mastermind.

"I'll drive them out to meet the fantasy family, but I'll take them to the middle of nowhere, perhaps to a forest," Oscar continues, his voice sounding more and more excited, "or a city they've never seen before. I'll leave them, then, on the side of the road like unwanted puppies."

"That's awful!" Ms. Young says.

But a moment later, her voice softer now, she adds, "When can we do it?"

# ~3~

"They can't get away with this," Hansen says when Gracie appears a few minutes later at their bunk bed in the dormitory.

"Sure they can. They get away with everything," Gracie says, sighing. She climbs into the top bunk and stares at the ceiling. Just inches from her face, nails poke through the bare wood beams holding up the rickety roof.

"But don't worry," Gracie continues, a mischievous smile forming on her cheeks. "I have a plan."

"Tell me," Hansen whispers, poking his head out from his bed to look up at his sister on the bunk above him.

Her hand sticks out from the top bunk and opens, dropping something. Hansen quickly catches what falls.

"A phone," Hansen says, turning it over in his hands. "Where did you get it?"

"Stole it from Oscar. He left it on kitchen counter," Gracie says.

"Who are we going to call? The police?" Hansen asks.

"Nah," Gracie says. She rolls onto her side. "The nasty lady is just going to tell the police we ran away. Why bother?"

"Then who?" Hansen says.

"No one," she says. "The phone has GPS.

They'll leave us, and we'll use the GPS to get back. Easy."

"Ha!" Hansen says. He pokes at the phone's touch screen, looking at all the maps and apps. "Good one, sis."

"Thank you," Gracie says. She smiles.

The sun is up now, barely over the horizon, hidden behind blocks and blocks of apartments and office buildings.

Hansen takes a deep breath and puts his head on his pillow. "Any second now . . ." he whispers.

Gracie nods.

The dormitory door slams open.

"Rise and shine, children!" Ms. Young's voice wobbles through the huge, sparsely furnished room. The lights flicker on and shine too bright. Beds creak as boys and girls sit up and rub their eyes or roll over, desperately clinging to the dreams they'd been having. The dreams were, no doubt, more pleasant than the reality to which they've just awoken.

"All of you, get down to breakfast," says Ms. Young, and before the commotion of children yapping and dressing and dragging their feet across the cold wood floors can begin, she adds in a piercing voice: "Except the twins! You two—get your coats."

All eyes slide in our direction. We keep our faces like stone.

Gracie drops down from the top bunk. Hansen stands and passes Gracie her coat. Hand in hand, we walk toward the door and the flickering light from the hallway seeping into our dark dormitory on this gloomy, gray morning.

"Oscar!" Ms. Young calls down the lighted hallway when we reach her.

He comes jogging toward us a few moments later, wearing his green work jumpsuit and shaking his head.

"I've lost my phone," Oscar says, panting. "I can't understand it."

"I'm sure it'll turn up," says Ms. Young, her smile straining against her cheeks like knives in a plastic shopping bag.

She turns back to face us. "Hansen. Gracie," she says, bending her back and rounding her shoulders as she always does when she talks to children. "I have some very exciting news for you."

We hardly listen. We know all about the fantasy family and the little drive Oscar will take us on this morning.

When she's done, Gracie says, "Should we pack?"

"Oh, no," Ms. Young says. She even puts a hand on Gracie's shoulder. She sounds too delighted. "You'll just be meeting the couple today. You won't be moving in with them yet!" She forces a twinkle of a laugh.

"That's right," says Oscar. "Just a little

get-together this morning." Oscar has the most ridiculous southern twang, but only sometimes.

*He does it to seem friendly*, Gracie thinks as loud as she can. *I hate him.*

Hansen glances at Gracie and nods the tiniest bit.

And with a hand of Oscar's on each of our shoulders, his stout figure between us, we walk down the hallway under the long fluorescent lights.

At the end of the hall, he pushes open the metal door for us and leads the way down the stairs to the big front doors, which are always locked.

Oscar pulls the long chain of keys from the little retractor on his belt. He hunches over the bunch as if our knowing which key opens this door would be a huge tragedy. He selects one and opens the door, letting in the blowing snow and frigid air.

We move closer together, Hansen and Gracie, and Gracie puts her arm around Hansen's waist.

Oscar hardly pauses in the doorway. He stomps down the icy, powder-coated steps and toward his car—a huge blue two-door with a torn brown ragtop.

The passenger-side door squeaks and whines in an awful way as Oscar pulls it open. He pushes the passenger's seat forward, and we climb into the huge backseat.

As Oscar walks around the front of the car, Gracie pokes the stolen phone, switches on the GPS to make sure it's working, and then shuts the display again before Oscar climbs into the driver's seat with a grunt.

"And here we go," he says, grinning at us in the rearview mirror, as if a flash of those crooked brown teeth would make us feel excited, or even comfortable.

Gracie shivers. *Hate,* she thinks.

Hansen puts his hand on hers on the vinyl seat between us. The huge car rumbles through the slick city streets toward the highway.

We don't resist when Oscar pulls us out of the backseat, nowhere near any house, nowhere near any neighborhood or city or town.

We get out and don't cry and don't yell as he climbs back into the driver's seat of the huge blue car. We stand in silence and watch as the car chugs down the lonely, snow covered road out of these woods, toward the city and the Lakeview Sunrise Group Home for Boys and Girls.

When he's way out of sight, Gracie pulls the phone from the pocket of her jacket and wakes it up. The little thinking wheel spins, the map zooms in, and we start to walk.

# ~4~

We don't give up easily. We don't tire quickly. We've known hunger and we've known long walks with nothing to keep going for, but we've still gone on.

We find the Lakeview Sunrise Group Home for Boys and Girls late the next night. The snow has stopped falling, but it covers the ground, almost glowing under the moonlight.

Before we climb the front stoop and ring the

bell, not even sure they'll let us in, Gracie pulls the phone from her pocket. With the tiniest sliver of battery life left, she makes a phone call.

"Please send a police car to the orphanage," she tells the operator.

The operator asks, "The Lakeview Sunrise Group Home?"

"Of course," Gracie says. "Two children have been mistreated."

Hansen nods and crosses his arms.

"Who is this?" the police want to know, but Gracie ends the call and drops the phone onto the cement sidewalk. She lifts her heavy winter boot and brings it down hard, once, twice, three times, till the phone's glass screen is a cracked mess and the circuits and wires are spilling out, destroyed.

She looks at Hansen, and Hansen climbs the steps and presses his finger against the doorbell. He holds it there so the buzzing tone (so rarely rung, but so annoying to Ms. Young when it is) drones on and on.

Before long, Oscar's heavy, plodding footsteps echo from behind the front doors. His keys jangle. The doors open. His jaw drops when he sees us.

"We found your phone," Hansen says.

Gracie laughs. We push past the man and into the orphanage.

# ~5~

It's a couple of hours later, and we're in our beds, lying awake and still seething, when the doorbell rings again. We smile as we hear Ms. Young's tired feet drag down the hall. Soon Oscar's clomping boots join her.

"Let's go see who it is," Gracie whispers as she drops down from the top bunk.

Hansen sighs, but he follows.

We stalk across the dormitory floor in our

bare feet and pajamas, and then down the hallway to the top of the drafty stairway. The steps are ice cold and covered in wintery grit, but we go down and wait around the corner as Oscar opens the front door.

"Is there something we can help you with, officers?" he says.

We exchange a look, our eyes bright with anticipation. We're thrilled. We dart out from the corner and the shadows and toward the front door, despite the chilly gusts pushing past the police officers and into the home.

The one in uniform is young, and he has a friendly, open face. He spots us and lightly elbows the woman beside him.

She's not in a police uniform, and we think for a moment that she's with child protective services. Maybe she's even here to do a full inspection and then shut this place down forever.

She produces a badge, though, and

suddenly she's nothing so wonderful. She's another police officer.

She explains they got a call from Oscar's phone number. Four sets of grown-up eyes turn to look at us.

Hansen swallows hard and takes a step back.

Gracie thinks, as loud as she can: *hate*.

"We called," Gracie says. "That man left us in the middle of a field to die." She points to Oscar. "We had to walk back. It took almost two days."

The uniformed officer's eyebrows go up in surprise. The woman beside him twists her mouth and narrows her eyes. She looks at Oscar.

"These are the two children who ran away," he says.

The woman nods slowly and pulls a pad of paper and a pencil from her coat pocket.

"Hansen and Grace," she says, looking them up and down.

"We didn't run away," Gracie says, stepping closer to the grown-ups by the door.

*Stop,* Hansen thinks. *We should go back to bed. Right now.*

*No,* Gracie thinks, twisting to face Hansen. She pushes the word at him.

"They wanted us to die," Gracie says. "They left us in the middle of nowhere. They should go to jail."

Oscar clicks his tongue and shakes his head, looking down at the floor. *What a shame,* he seems to say. *The girl is so sad and angry that she's invented such an obvious lie.*

Ms. Young steps closer to Gracie and bends in front of her, the same way she had when she told us about our fantasy family out in the suburbs, desperate for twins just like us.

"We're not angry with you," Ms. Young

says sweetly. "But calling the police was going too far."

Gracie clenches her teeth, and we're not sure that she won't pull back a fist and use it on Ms. Young's chin.

But Ms. Young stands up straight and faces the police officers again.

"I'm very sorry you had to come out at this hour," she says. "The girl stole Oscar's phone the other day. She must have called the station on that. We just found it smashed up outside the home."

"We have to check these things out," says the woman officer. "You understand." She glances at us and frowns.

"Of course, of course," Oscar says, shuffling the police officers out of the doorway and back into the cold middle of the night. He and Ms. Young look pleasant standing in the doorway, each with a hand on one of our shoulders, their grips a bit too strong.

"No harm done!" Oscar shouts after them.

The officers wave goodbye from the driveway. The door to the orphanage closes with a heavy thud and click.

# ~6~

Ms. Young and Oscar both turn slowly to face us again. She stands up as straight as a flagpole, with her chin high and her eyes cast down on us.

He hunches, his hands open and out to us, like he might grab us each by the throat and toss us out into the snow.

But he won't—not right away.

"It was the phone, wasn't it?" he says. He

takes a slow, heavy step toward us. "That's how you got back." He takes another step.

"Take it easy, Oscar," Ms. Young says. "This is why we took precautions."

Oscar stands up straight—or as straight as he can—and bites his lip.

We want to go back to bed now.

Hansen shuffles backward till his back hits the railing of the stairwell. Gracie catches Hansen's wrist and pulls him closer to her.

"If we hadn't reported you two as runaways immediately," Ms. Young hisses at us, "those officers would have had to investigate fully."

"We're going to bed," Gracie says.

"By all means," Ms. Young says, her voice dripping with hate.

We hurry up the staircase toward the flickering light of the hallway and run through the dormitory to our bunk bed by the cold window.

Half of the kids are sitting up, wide awake in the dark, waiting to hear the news. "What's happening?" they ask us. "Where were you?" some want to know.

"Why'd you run away?" asks the littlest one, a five-year-old boy they brought here just a few days ago. He's still too stupid to see the truth about this place.

We don't answer any of them. We almost never do.

We get back into bed, and somehow we fall asleep.

We dream about a house. It's far away from here, set atop a soft green slope. It's a white house with storm-gray shutters, or it's a pale blue house with red shutters, or it's a butter-yellow house with black shutters, and it's encircled by a wood fence.

An apple tree crouches in the front yard, and it dangles little sweet apples, colored red and green. We pick as many as we can carry in our upturned T-shirt fronts. And when we're done, our mother opens the front door and calls us inside.

But we wake up, and it's only Ms. Young standing over us.

*7*

She takes us from our beds. Oscar is there. They take us by our collars and drag us from the room before the lights click on, before the other kids can even open their eyes and sit up. Not that that would have helped.

They don't pretend this morning. There are no stories about a couple who'd like to meet us. No lies about the perfect little house in the suburbs.

There's no breakfast, no packing of clothes, and there are certainly no goodbyes.

There's only the backseat of Oscar's giant, smelly car. The doors slamming. The motor coughing and chugging.

We're on the highway again, and this time he takes us farther. We don't recognize the road signs. The farmhouses and the silos are unfamiliar after living in the city.

We shouldn't have smashed the phone. We shouldn't have called the police. We shouldn't have argued with them. We should have been sweeter children.

Gracie keeps her eyes out the window, reading signs, looking for landmarks, tracking the sun on the horizon.

*It's no good,* Hansen thinks. *We won't get back twice. He'll be sure of that.*

Gracie wipes the back of her hand across her eyes. Hansen puts a hand on her back.

"Why don't you just kill us?" Hansen snarls toward the front seat.

Oscar chuckles. "I'm not an animal," he replies.

~ 8 ~

He leaves us deep inside the woods this time. A place we've never seen.

We stand at the side of the road and watch the huge blue car shake and rocket away, coughing out gray and black smoke as it drives down the dirty country highway, covered in road salt and snow-filled potholes.

There are no billboards or road signs. No telephone poles or farmhouses.

All we can see is this road, this forest, and, once in a while, a logging truck passing by.

We hope his car breaks down. We hope he ends up stranded in these woods, too.

"Which way?" Hansen asks. Gracie takes Hansen's hand. We start to walk.

We keep to the road and follow it as it goes on and on.

When the sun sets, it sets behind us, and we're pretty sure we've been walking in the wrong direction.

"I don't care," says Gracie. "I don't want to go back."

"I don't either," says Hansen.

Ahead of us, far on the horizon, city lights twinkle as the sun sets.

"It's a different city," Gracie says. There's almost hope in her voice. We walk through the night.

Soon, a sliver of light emerges from the

horizon, and the road we're on is well paved and marked with a bright yellow line down the middle.

There's a gas station on the corner up ahead. There's a tiny old restaurant. There are homes now . . . on this road and on littler roads that shoot off of it like baby branches on a sapling tree.

Around us, the world is changing from a forbidding forest to a plain country lane.

Eventually it changes again, from a small farming town to a lively and bright suburb, and our road—the one we've been walking on forever it seems—has become a tree-lined boulevard. There are sidewalks, shoveled and clear of snow.

It's midmorning now, and the locals are out. They're hurrying between the post office and the hardware store. They're shuffling between the coffee shop and their nice-looking cars, which are lined up neatly along the curbside.

They're juggling toddlers and groceries and peppermint hot chocolates with whipped cream.

Some of them look at us, but they don't really see us. Some of them see us, and they quickly look away, turning back to their groceries or their coffee thermoses. Some of them see us, and they stare.

Everyone wonders why we're here—we can tell. They wonder what happened to us.

*They'll take us back,* Gracie thinks. *I don't want to go back.*

Hansen takes her hand. He leads us off the main boulevard, under elm trees that hang over snow-blanketed, narrow streets, past driveways and front yards strewn with snowmen, Christmas displays, and red and blue and pink and green sleds.

This is a place we'd like to live.

We almost expect the house we dreamed about, with its wooden fence and perfect apple

tree, to appear each time we turn a corner. But we don't say it out loud.

Before too long, we've walked the entire width of this little suburb, and we still haven't found our dream house.

In front of us is a highway that leads into the city. The city sits on the horizon to the east, gray and smoggy and gloomy.

But we know it's not the city we came from, at least.

"What should we do?" Gracie says. She wishes as hard she can, because she wants to find that house—the house with the big, friendly apple tree.

She wants to find that house and knock on its door and go inside and stay there forever, picking apples, baking delicious desserts, and sleeping in warm, comfortable beds.

She wants it to be our home.

"It was a dream," Hansen says gently.

And Hansen leads us to the city, because in the city we can survive.

## ~9~

The city feels colder than the suburb did.

We arrive tired, our clothes torn and wet, icy at the hems that hang past our feet, picking up mud and snow as we trudge along.

We're hungry. We both know it. But Gracie says it out loud, and it becomes that much more real.

It's night again, and we can't remember the last time we ate. It was back at the orphanage, of course. And that was days ago now. Our stomachs rumble as we walk.

Gracie is crying again. She wipes the back of her hand under her nose and sniffles hard.

Dirty snowbanks are piled high on the sides of the city streets. But there's a courthouse, a city hall, and even a sports stadium nearby. And in the center of this new city, the night bustles and gives us hope.

Restaurants and cafés and bars, with grown-ups pouring out of open doorways, send heat from inside out into the street.

Everyone here seems rich, cheerful, and loud. Everyone is eating and drinking and celebrating.

"I'll get us some food," Hansen says as they pass by a restaurant. He steps away from Gracie.

Hansen slips into the crowd of people outside the restaurant. The air around us smells like French fries and hot sauce and pickles.

He pushes through them. The workers hardly notice he's there, it's so busy.

They don't notice when he finds a table whose diners are up and mingling on the dance floor.

Hansen grabs two burgers from the table, wraps them in napkins and jams them into the pockets of his coat, looking around carefully to make sure no one can see him.

Gracie smiles and pulls in her lips. "Get the fries," she whispers.

Hansen snatches the French fries off the table and stuffs them under his armpit inside his coat.

He's pushing his way through the crowd again and toward Gracie when a shout rises up behind him. "Hey!"

Someone must have seen him snatch the fries.

We gasp. We hold our breath.

Hansen keeps moving. A pair of hands grabs his shoulders, so he pulls away, leaving his coat and our dinner behind.

*Run,* he screams in our minds. Gracie steps slowly away from the crowd as the people grow enraged.

Hands claw at Hansen, but he pushes through them. His clothes tear. His skin, still raw from a day and a half of walking in the frigid cold, burns and stings with pain as their fingernails scratch violently at his arms.

Some people even try to trip him, sticking their feet in front of his as he tries to escape.

The crowd swells through the doorway, catching Hansen in the middle of the group like he's a fallen surfer caught in a huge wave.

Then, not knowing what else to do, Gracie balls her hands into fists and shrieks.

Everything stops.

The crowd loosens its grip on Hansen and

everyone turns their attention to Gracie. All the crowd's shouts and curses of angry rage die out, so we can only hear the music from within the restaurant.

Hansen moves toward his sister. The crowd, as if under Gracie's spell, lets him.

Hansen takes Gracie's hand. We run from the restaurant, past a dozen more just like it, and we keep running for blocks and blocks.

Soon the streets are cobblestone and the buildings are quiet and dark, stout warehouses and factories set against the unfriendly, charcoal-colored sky.

Only one faint light shines in this part of the city: a blue globe on a steel post to mark the entrance to the local police station.

"They can help us," Hansen says.

We're so hungry. We're cold and tired.

It would be so easy to go inside. To give them our names. To sit down. To ask for a doughnut and two cups of hot chocolate. They would help us.

Even if they believed we were runaways. They'd help us.

We walk between parked police cars and motorcycles and stop at the bottom of the station's stoop.

We can see the officers inside, laughing and playing cards, doing paperwork and drinking coffee.

"If we go in," Gracie says, giving Hansen's hand an extra squeeze, "they'll bring us right back to the orphanage."

Hansen takes a deep breath.

"I don't want to go back," Gracie says, facing her brother.

"We'll starve," he says. We're so hungry. Hansen's coat is gone. We'll freeze.

Hansen sighs. "But we can't go back to the orphanage," he says.

So we turn our backs on the police station and walk.

# ~10~

We walk until the sun is coming up in front of us. There's a wide river on the city's east side, so we walk along the river road until we reach a high, lighted bridge, alive and shaking with early-morning commuter trains and highway traffic.

We hold onto the railings of the pedestrian path as we cross, wary of the shaking steel that is holding us up.

"It's supposed to shake," Hansen says, and we believe it, but it doesn't help to know.

On the far side of the bridge, the city is gone, and there are trees and small homes and gas stations and a post office, just like there had been in the suburb before the city.

The road bends around and becomes a highway. We can't walk safely there, so we take a turn after the post office and find ourselves on a narrow street, with cars parked all along one side.

There are little white homes with dark blue shutters and fences of wrought iron and white-painted wood.

We stop at the far end of the block, where the street becomes a wide cul-de-sac on a gentle slope.

At the top of the slope sits a house that we both recognize at once. The sight of it makes us catch our breath and grab one another's hand.

The house is pale blue-gray, with bright white shutters and a door so boldly red against the snowy landscape that it makes our eyes water.

A gate sits open in the center of the wooden fence that encloses the front yard, which is covered in untrodden snow.

There's the friendly-looking apple tree reaching toward the sun in the clear sky, waving its supple branches back and forth in the winter wind.

"It can't be real," Hansen says, his voice cautious. But it's right there in front of us, just like we dreamed it.

"It is," Gracie says, facing her brother and taking his hands. "We should go in. We should ring the bell!"

Hansen shakes his head.

We're anxious. We're afraid. But we feel excited. We feel jubilant.

"Something doesn't seem right here," Hansen says slowly, looking at the house suspiciously. "Dreams don't come true like this, Gracie."

"Not ever?" she says, her eyes pleading and her lips blue with cold.

We don't have to decide. We don't have to argue.

Because just then, the front door of our dream house swings open and a woman appears in the doorway.

She isn't our mother. But she's smiling, and her face is open and kind, and she says, "Good morning, children. Please, come in out of the cold."

So we do.

And there's soup for us, and there's ice cream afterward, and she washes our clothes and mends our pants. The woman even has a new coat for Hansen. She lets us each take a bath in water so warm it makes our toes tingle.

When it's dark and we're warm and full from eating, she puts us to bed, too. We sleep in beds so fluffy and warm that we feel we could sleep for days, waking only to eat hot soup and smell fresh apple pie baking in the oven.

We thank her as we drift away.

Since we know we're in our dream house, tonight we sleep, for the first time we can remember, with no dreams at all.

* * *

When we wake up, the floor is cold and the beds are gone, and Hansen is in a cage and Gracie's ankles and wrists are shackled with metal rings and rope.

The woman is with us, directly across the low-ceilinged, cement-floor room. There are no windows and it is damp and cold.

She says, "Good morning, darlings. Did you sleep well?" Then she laughs an evil laugh as she climbs the steps out of the basement.

It's not our dream house after all. It's our nightmare.

# ~11~

We knew dreams didn't come true.
Hansen had even said it out loud. But we came inside anyway. When we saw her in the open doorway, we didn't care.

When she put her arms around us, smelling of apples and honey and lavender, nothing could have stopped us from going with her.

And now we're paying for our foolishness. For being willing to believe. For being babies.

Hansen sits on the floor of his cage, hugging his knees tight to his chest. His cheeks have been dry for a long time now.

The sobbing and screaming have done nothing more than leave his throat sore and dry and his dirty cheeks streaked where tears spilled from his eyes.

Gracie leans against the bars outside the cage. She had cried along with him.

We wonder why. *Why is Hansen in the cage, but Gracie outside? Why is Gracie in leg irons, her hands tied in ropes?*

But we don't need to wonder for long. Once we are silent, the woman floats back downstairs.

"You've calmed down," she says as she walks across the cement floor. "Perhaps now we can speak."

*We have nothing to say to her,* we think. *Don't say anything to her.*

"You're both so hungry and so skinny," the woman says.

She shakes her head, like it's a great shame that we've been through so much, like she cares about us.

"I can't have two skinny weaklings, not for my needs." It turns out the woman does care—kind of.

"Gracie, darling," she says, and she runs a hand over Gracie's head, pushing her hair back and tucking it behind her ear.

We shiver at the touch. *We hate her.*

"You will be my helper," she says, folding her hands together and smiling down at Gracie. "You will clean, and you will wash, and you will learn to cook."

*Don't answer her,* we think.

"You," she says, turning to the cage.

Hansen shrinks like a pet gerbil, pushing his back against the farthest corner. She only smiles at him, lets out a little giggle, like he really is a pet gerbil.

"I have something much more important in mind for you."

*Don't answer her!* we think, but Gracie's eyes are watering again, and she can't resist.

"Why don't you let him out?" she says. "He can help me clean."

The woman frowns at her, the sort of frown that has a smile inside it. "No, no," she says. She waves the idea away. "That would never do."

*You shouldn't have answered her,* Hansen thinks.

"We work better as a team," Gracie says.

*Stop,* Hansen thinks.

"I'm afraid," the woman says, "I've seen too many boys attempt housework and fail miserably. No, no. They make much better meat than maid."

"You're lying," Hansen says, glaring at her. "You're just trying to scare us."

But the woman doesn't seem to hear him. Her eyes and mind are far away. "The last time I had a brother and sister down here," she says, pacing slowly in front of his cage, a delighted and wicked smile forming on her lips, "she created the most perfect Béarnaise sauce. She had no idea that a few hours later I'd pour it over her brother's glistening golden-brown carcass."

*She's a monster,* we think. *We have to get away.* But we can't.

The woman claps twice and brings her heels together as she faces Gracie. "My dear," she says, "let's get you started out front."

"Someone will see me," Gracie says. "They'll see me wearing these *things,*" she says, shaking her shackles and ropes at the evil woman, "and they'll set me free. They'll call the police, you know."

"And you'll end up right back where you started," the woman says.

We almost gasp. *How does she know?* we think.

"I know a couple of runaways when I see them," the woman goes on. "Besides, what kind of miserable witch do you take me for? With the charms I've placed on this house, any passersby—not that we'll have any on a frigid morning like this—would wave good morning and wish you the best of the season."

*Impossible,* we think. But she continues, "They wouldn't see your ropes. They wouldn't see your leg irons. They wouldn't even see the state of your clothes or the knots in your hair or the bruise on your cheek. My spells can't be broken until I reverse them."

Gracie reaches for her cheek before she remembers the ropes. It's an awkward motion to test the pain under her eye.

She can't remember when she got the

bruise. *The witch must have given it to me,* she thinks.

"And don't think about running off, either," the witch says as she heads for the stairs. "As long as I'm alive, this house and yard are a fortress as far as you two are concerned."

*Then we'll kill her,* we think. *Somehow, we'll kill her.*

* * *

For the next several days, we are strong.

Gracie works hard. She cries, but she is fed well and she manages to sleep a few hours.

Hansen, still in his cage, refuses to eat more than a few bites of bread or a spoonful of rice.

The witch fumes at him, pushing bowls of ice cream into his cage. Hansen lets them melt into soup and pushes the bowls back, still full, the spoons untouched.

She brings him plates of frosted cupcakes in every color of the rainbow. Hansen turns them upside down on the plates, showing off the brown-stained paper cups. Cupcakes don't look delicious from the bottom. He smears the different colors of frosting together into a color no one would want to eat.

"You can't hold out forever," the witch says, crouching beside the cage and sneering at him, her eyes glinting.

But Hansen is sure he can. We're both sure.

And every time Hansen stomps a bacon sandwich till it's flat and dirty and marked with the pattern from the sole of his shoe, or dumps a plate of fries on the floor and paints the cage bars with ketchup, or just sits back and watches a bowl of macaroni and cheese grow cold and congealed, the fork nearly standing upright, Gracie smiles.

She might be bent in the kitchen, scrubbing the floor. She might be in the back bedrooms, polishing the old wood furniture. She might be pushing a shovel up and down the bumpy driveway, covered with new snowfall for the fourth time this week.

But she smiles, because she knows we're beating the witch.

# ~12~

It is our seventh morning in the house. Gracie is sent to the attic with a broom.

"It's full of dust," the witch says, ushering her up the narrow, steep staircase hidden in the closet in the back bedroom. She closes the closet door and heads for the basement.

*She's coming,* Gracie thinks. *She's bringing breakfast.*

Hansen looks up. His head aches. His body

is covered in welts and bruises from living and sleeping and ranting in his cage.

He's hungry. He's so hungry.

Gracie feels Hansen's hunger, too. She clutches her belly as she works. She eats simple meals—lumpy oatmeal, heels of stale, hard bread, scraps of dry meat.

Hansen enjoys the tastes whenever Gracie eats, but it just makes him more hungry. Gracie wants to cry whenever she has a meal. She knows Hansen can taste the miserable stuff. But no matter how much Gracie eats, Hansen will still be hungry afterward.

"Rise and shine, my little roast of lamb," the witch says in a menacing tone.

She walks slowly. She always walks slowly. Not tired. Not gloomy. More like a helium balloon on its gentle way down, swimming on a breeze no one else can feel.

This morning, she carries a plate of toast.

Just toast. It's not even buttered. She places it beside the cage and steps back.

There's a chair not far from the cage where she sits to watch Hansen eat—or, more likely, to watch him not eat.

"If you don't eat," the witch says, crossing her arms and legs and smiling at him, "you'll starve."

He looks up at her, his hunger and exhaustion making his vision blurry and bright. He thinks again about how beautiful she is, how beautiful she smelled when she embraced them in a hug.

He even remembers how much he loved her—really loved her—when she first opened the front door to them that happy morning just one week ago.

"More to the point," she adds, her voice playful and sharp, "*I'll* starve."

*We hate her.*

"I don't care," Hansen says. "I'll waste away if I have to."

"You'd leave your poor sister all alone?" the witch says.

Hansen swallows.

*Don't answer,* Gracie thinks.

"She's been eating quite well, you know," the witch says as she stands. "Sure, she's working hard and no doubt her knees are bruised and sore and her hands are callused and cramped. But she eats three meals a day. She often has seconds."

"It won't work," Hansen says. Gracie smiles for him. "You can't make me any more hungry than I am."

His throat is dry and his voice is tired, but he goes on. "You can't make me jealous, because Gracie is my whole world, and I couldn't be jealous of her if she was taking bubble baths every day and eating all the food I've turned down."

"What makes you think she isn't?" the witch says, leaning forward.

*Don't answer,* Gracie thinks. *She doesn't know about us—not really. She doesn't know we're connected.*

Hansen crosses his arms and bites his lower lip. He looks at the wall.

The witch comes up next to the cage, right next to Hansen, and before he can skitter away, she takes hold of his wrist through the metal bars.

"It doesn't matter," she hisses in his ear. "I've decided to let you rot, to let you die here in your own filth. I'll be happy to never come down to this basement again."

"You'll have nothing to eat," Hansen says, and his voice and throat are so dry it sounds as if he's already begun to decompose.

"Do you think only boys are made of meat?" the witch says.

Hansen's skin tingles and goes cold. Two stories up, in a low-ceilinged dark room, with a rag in her hand, Gracie shivers.

And we think: *hate.*

# ~13~

At noon the same day, Gracie descends the attic stairs. Her legs are sore and the stairway is steep and her irons are heavy, so it's slowgoing.

She coughs and sneezes, too. The attic was indeed a plague of dust, and as she worked, much of it found her nose and throat and lungs.

But Gracie would like to stay in the attic

forever, because she knows what the witch has planned for her now.

The witch is waiting for her, sitting on the edge of the loveseat, the one with the wooden legs that Gracie had polished for an hour only a few mornings ago. She's smiling a tiny, cruel sort of smile.

"All done?" the witch says.

Gracie doesn't answer her. She just stands there, her wrists bound together in front of her, a few dirty brown rags dangling from one hand that is just as dirty.

"Go to the kitchen, then," the witch says. She keeps her eyes cast downward as she brushes lint from her lap. "I'm having trouble with the oven."

Gracie shuffles past the witch, her irons clanking and the wet rags in her hand slapping against her thigh. The witch grabs her wrist to stop her.

"Take the long matches out from the

cupboard," the witch says, and her voice doesn't tinkle like it sometimes does. Instead it crackles like a fire. It doesn't bubble like a cool stream. It sizzles like a juicy slice of meat dropped into a hot frying pan.

The witch lets go of Gracie's wrist and stands up. She follows Gracie down the main staircase and into the kitchen.

The witch leans on the counter as Gracie pulls the box of long matches from the cupboard, eyeing her carefully.

"Do you know how to light it?" the witch says, a little too eagerly. "Do you know where the pilot light is?"

Gracie pulls a single long match from the box and closes the box again.

The witch tugs on the heavy oven door. It creaks and groans as it falls open.

"It's in the back of the oven," the witch says. "You'll have to lean all the way in."

*This is it,* we think.

*Don't lean in,* Hansen thinks. *She's lying. The pilot is lit.*

Gracie strikes the match against the box and reaches her rope-bound arms along the wall of the oven, straining and stretching to get her hands into the depths of the huge contraption while staying steady on her feet.

"No," the witch snarls. "You'll never reach it like that. Climb inside."

Gracie grunts and stretches farther. "I can reach it," she says.

"Just climb in!"

Gracie sighs and stands. "I don't know what you mean," she says. "And I can't find the pilot light anyway."

"It's right there!" the witch snaps. "You have to climb in."

"Show me," Gracie says.

Hansen laughs.

*Shh,* Gracie says, barely able to hold in her own laughter.

The witch narrows her eyes at Gracie.

*We hate her.*

The witch brings up her fist, tight and hot, and it begins to glow.

*It's evil magic,* we think.

She shines her magic light toward the back of the dark oven.

"I can't see it," Gracie says. "It's in the back?"

The witch ducks her head and leans into the oven, reaching her glowing hand toward the far corner. "It's right there," she says, frustrated.

"Oh," Gracie says. She quietly moves around behind the witch.

*Do it,* thinks Hansen. *Do it now.*

Gracie leans down. She takes a step back and charges, shoulder down, into the witch's backside.

The witch loses her footing and falls face-first into the oven.

"What are you doing?!" she shrieks. Her voice is now a fiery rage that seems to tear at her throat as she pushes it through, and it echoes off the oven's steel walls.

We're laughing now, both of us. We're laughing loudly and madly.

Gracie reaches her bound hands to the door and shoves it up, sending the witch deeper into the huge oven. She slams the door closed and throws the lock.

*How hot does it go?* Hansen thinks.

Gracie scans the control panel and turns the oven knob as high as it will go—550 degrees Fahrenheit. Then she sees the "broil" setting, and turns the knob there.

She grins then, and Hansen grins in his cage in the basement, and she turns the knob to "clean."

The witch bangs on the walls of the oven as it begins to heat up. "Let me out of here!" she screams.

It's her truest voice, her most vile voice. It's the voice of a demon. It's the voice of the devil himself.

The witch slams her body into the oven's door. Her voice is more like a growl now, like the violent rage of a wild animal, of a monster.

The oven shakes. The kitchen shakes. The witch is trying to break through the oven door.

*Don't let her out!* Hansen screams through our minds.

Gracie pushes her body against the door. With all her strength she holds the door closed, the witch's screams piercing Gracie's ears till they've nearly deafened her.

She can feel the heat pressing through the door, and the witch's screams grow still louder. The kitchen is filling with smoke and the acrid smell of the broiling witch.

"Is it almost done?!" Gracie screams over the din.

"Yes!" Hansen screams back from his cage in the basement. He's on his feet now, his hands gripping the bars of his cage in anticipation. "Hold on a little longer!"

The screams begin to waver and dry, like they're turning to dust, turning to ash. They soften. They begin to plead. They are no longer screams.

Instead, Gracie hears the woman's false voice—the one she used to welcome Hansen and Gracie into her house, with apple on her breath and love in her arms.

# ~14~

Gracie begins to cry. She pulls her shoulder back from the door and puts her hand on the lock.

*Stop!* Hansen thinks. *She's a witch.*

Gracie shakes away the thoughts.

"We hate her!" Hansen screams from the basement. It doesn't matter who hears him now. "We'll kill her!"

Gracie pulls her hand from the lock like it's

a rattlesnake, and as the begging from inside the oven dies out, she runs from the kitchen to the basement steps.

There's only silence now. Silence and thick gray smoke and the nauseating smell of burnt witch.

"Hansen!" Gracie shouts, her voice a strange mix of gleeful and grotesque as she goes down the steps as awkward as ever, her ankle irons clanking between her feet, almost making her fall.

Grasping the banister with her bound hands is nearly impossible, but she moves faster than she has in a week.

"She's gone," Hansen says. He's on his feet at the front of the cage. He's holding the bars and he's actually smiling. His cheeks are even sore. We both feel it, and it makes us smile even more.

"Let me out," he says, but at the bottom of the steps, Gracie stops suddenly, remembering something. She starts to speak, but she doesn't have to.

"She had the keys," Hansen says, his smile dropping away.

Gracie almost panics. *Can we live our lives here, with Hansen in a cage and with Gracie bound in irons?*

"No," she says. "I'll find them."

She turns and clang-clangs her way up the stairs. She stands in front of the oven, still hot, and takes a deep breath. "Okay," she says. "She's dead."

Gracie pulls open the oven's lock and the appliance groans and clunks. She opens the oven door, half expecting the woman—her face mutilated from the heat—to reach for her and pull her inside. Instead she finds a pile of ashes on the floor of the oven and, in the center of the oven, a ring of keys.

She grabs a rag from the counter, because the keys are still too hot to touch, and wraps it around the ash-covered key ring. Then she hurries back downstairs, almost falling as she goes.

Unlocking the cage with the keys wrapped in the rag is difficult, but Gracie finally throws open the cage's big barred door.

"Now me," she says.

Hansen is weak. He manages to pick up the keys wrapped in the rag, but he can't turn the lock in his sister's ankle irons. Gracie puts her hands on Hansen's and we turn the key together. The irons fall away, clanking on the basement's cement floor.

Hansen is strong enough to undo the ropes. With us both free, he feels strong enough for anything.

But for now, we are happy to throw our arms around each other.

# ~15~

She's dead, and her charms are wearing off. It doesn't happen all at once, though, like we thought it would. Instead, little bits of the enchantment change or disappear completely, one at a time.

First it's the house. What once appeared to be a beautifully decorated bungalow begins to crumble.

Inside, the wallpaper is peeling where it

had been pristine only hours ago. The antique furniture Gracie polished tirelessly for hours is only a heap of broken junk now.

Out front, the apple tree is a gnarled and ghastly thing. Its branches are bare and ragged, looking more like the deformed limbs of a mythical beast than a friendly fruit tree.

We rest. We eat. We sleep.

But the only bed in the house is the witch's, which we now realize is not a beautiful four-poster with a thick and fluffy mattress and downy comforters as it had appeared when the charms still held. Now we see that it's an iron basin filled with mud and blood.

*She was a beast,* we think.

But we wouldn't sleep in her bed even if it were the most comfortable bed in the world. Not for anything.

So we sleep on the floor, but not in the basement. We'll never go back to the basement.

We have to keep an eye on the front of the house as well. With the witch's charms gone, the neighbors have begun to notice the house.

It's crumbling, after all. And it's finally beginning to look like the haunted house it's always been.

The neighbors don't stop by . . . not yet. But soon, we know, they'll get curious. First the children will start to throw rocks at the windows. Then the grown-ups will silently wonder what happened to the woman who had lived here. One brave adult might come knock on the door.

Eventually, someone will call the city. And they'll come condemn the building, maybe even knock it down. We'll end up back at the home.

So we work. We clean every inch and repair everything that's broken. Gracie is good at this by now, and Hansen is better at housework than the witch predicted.

Gracie is hunting for the source of an odor in the front closet while Hansen is fixing the big window in the living room.

Gracie finds a tiny door at the back of the closet, hidden by years of debris and dust. We force it open, Hansen wielding his screwdriver like a crowbar.

We gasp together. We've found the witch's treasure!

*Jewels,* Gracie thinks.

*Gold,* Hansen thinks.

And cash, too. She was a modern witch. We find bundled bills and checkbooks and even a pair of credit cards.

*We can survive here,* we think, and we run to the computer in the witch's office. Thankfully, the computer is not disguised as an enchanted cauldron anymore. It's a real PC with an Internet connection.

Before long, we've made adoption papers

and printed them out, complete with forged seals and signatures.

"Did she have a name?" Gracie says as we stare at the blank line, where the name of the adopting parent should be entered.

We don't know. So we give her one, and we finally have a last name: Appletree.

# ~16~

We spend most of our time alone now, in the witch's house. The neighbors don't stop by often, but when they do, we say, "Our mother is out. Can we help you?" or "Mom's napping. Can you come by another time?"

We enroll at the local high school, too. It's easy. We fill out all the forms and submit them online. We forge anything requiring signatures or doctor's notes.

By the time the spring semester starts—just days after we burned the witch to death—we have decent clothes, school supplies, and a place in the ninth grade.

We are nervous at first. We lie in our beds the night before our first day. We're sharing a room in the back of house, with two small beds pushed against opposite walls.

"I'm scared," Hansen says.

"It's what we've always dreamed of," Gracie says. "A perfect little house in a perfect little town. Going to school with other kids our age. We'll be safe and we'll be happy."

Hansen says, "Okay," but he still isn't sure. Neither of us is sure.

\* \* \*

We're in our first class on our first day. Our teacher is a grim man, middle-aged and tired-looking. He speaks to us and the rest of the students in clipped, angry sentences.

When the buzzer sounds to start the day and the semester and the rest of our educational lives, he calls over the conversations and greetings of the returning students.

"We have to welcome a couple of new kids to our class today," he says, and he motions for us to stand, so we do. "You're twins, aren't you?"

"Yes, sir," Gracie says.

Some of the kids giggle at that. They giggle because we've been raised to say things like "yes, sir" when we speak at all.

We decide to try not to speak.

"Where did you kids move from?" he says.

We glance at each other.

*Don't answer,* Hansen thinks.

But the teacher is looking at us, and his phony smile is growing stiffer and sterner.

"Did you hear me?" the teacher says.

Hansen coughs into his hand.

"When you're asked a question in my class," he says, his smile now totally gone and his face growing red, "I expect you to answer. Right away and truthfully."

"Yes, sir," Gracie says.

The rest of the class giggles again, and the teacher shakes his head, disappointed and horrible.

*We hate them,* we think. *We hate all of them.*

# Hansel
# and
# Gretel

• ★ • ★ •

The fairy tale known as Hansel and Gretel was first published by the Brothers Grimm in 1812. Parts of the story may have originated during the Great Famine in Europe in the early fourteenth century.

Hansel and Gretel are twins, the children of a poor woodcutter and their stepmother. In the midst of a famine, the stepmother convinces their father to abandon the twins in the woods because they eat too much.

They are left in the woods twice, and the first time they find their way home. The second time, they are left farther away in the forest, and they can't find their way back. Soon they come across a house made of cakes and candy. The twins begin to eat the house until an old woman emerges from it and invites them inside with promise of comfortable beds and delicious food.

The next morning, she forces Gretel to be her slave, and she locks Hansel in a cage, hoping to fatten him up to eat. One day, the witch prepares the oven for Hansel but decides she is hungry enough to eat Gretel, too. Before she can, Gretel shoves her into the oven, burning the witch alive.

The twins find the witch's jewels, pocket them, and eventually make their way home to their father, finding that their stepmother has died while they've been gone. The whole time they've been away, their father has felt awful for treating his children so cruelly. He is thrilled to see his children again. With the witch's fortune in hand, the family lives happily ever after.

# Tell your own twicetold Tale!

• ✱ • ✱ •

Choose one from each group, and write a story that combines all of the elements you've chosen.

A princess who is angry at her parents

A young man who doesn't know he's a prince

A witch who helps animals

A monster who travels the world

An apple tree

An old notebook

A silver spoon

A kaleidoscope

---

A home on a cliff

A tree house

A hut on the beach

A sailboat

---

A fairy godmother

A troll

A sorcerer

An elderly maid

---

A pony

A spider

A whale

A monkey

---

Boston in the 1600s

Southern California

A village in Ireland

Turkey

# about the author

Olivia Snowe lives between the falls, the forest, and the creek in Minneapolis, Minnesota.

# about the illustrator

Michelle Lamoreaux is an illustrator from southern Utah. She works with many publishers, agencies, and magazines throughout the US. She currently works out of Salt Lake City, Utah.